How Do Engineers Solve Problems?

 HOUGHTON MIFFLIN HARCOURT

PHOTOGRAPHY CREDITS: COVER ©Digital Vision/Getty Images; 3 (bl) ©Hans Peter Merten/Getty Images; 3 (br) ©D. Hurst/Alamy Images; 4 (b) ©Blue Jean Images/Alamy Images; 5 (br) ©Wealan Pollard/Alamy Images; 6 (br) ©Radius Images/Alamy Images; 7 (t) ©Image Source/Getty Images; 8 (b) ©GerryRousseau/Alamy Images; 9 (b) ©Sami Sarkis/Getty Images; 11 (br) ©Elena Elisseeva/Alamy Images

Printed in Mexico

ISBN: 978-0-544-07239-8

3 4 5 6 7 8 9 10 0908 21 20 19 18 17 16 15 14

4500469985   A B C D E F

Be an Active Reader!

Look for each word in yellow along with its meaning.

technology   engineer

environment   design process

Underlined sentences in the text answer these questions.

What is technology?

What technology do children use to get to school?

What classroom technology do you use?

How does technology affect our environment?

What do engineers do?

What is the design process?

How can the design process help you solve a problem?

What is technology?

Technology is made to meet needs. It finds answers to problems, too. It is all around us!

Cars get us from place to place. Long ago, people made cars using their hands. Today, people have help. They use machines. Machines help us make cars.

A telephone lets you talk to people. A washing machine washes your clothes. Other machines make food hot or cold. What technology do you use?

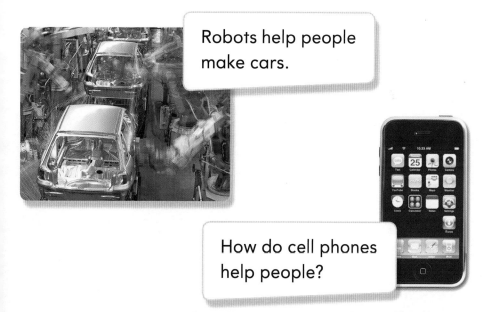

Robots help people make cars.

How do cell phones help people?

What technology do children use to get to school?

Some children take a car to school. An engine makes the car move. The wheel helps the car turn. Brakes make it stop. A seat belt keeps people safe.

Many children ride bikes to school. How do children move their bikes? They use their feet. Bikes have handles. They help children turn their bikes. Children wear helmets. Helmets keep children's heads safe.

A seat belt will keep you safe in an accident.

What classroom technology do you use?

You can find a lot of technology in a classroom. A computer is technology. It can help you learn. You can find out about animals. You can use a computer to write a report.

A whiteboard is classroom technology. You can write words on it. You can draw pictures, too.

Think about other technology you use. A pencil helps you write. Scissors help you cut paper. A thumbtack holds up your work.

You can write on a whiteboard.

You can cut paper with scissors.

5

How does technology affect our environment?

The environment is all the living and nonliving things in a place. Living things are plants, animals, and people. Nonliving things are items we use.

Sometimes technology hurts plants and animals. It is not good when we use a lot of plastic. It becomes trash. But we can recycle it. Then it is turned into something new. Or, we can reuse it. Wash a plastic cup and use it again!

Plastic can be recycled into something new.

Some engineers make plans for buildings.

What do engineers do?

An engineer is a scientist. Engineers use math and science to help people. They solve problems in their job.

Engineers make plans. A plan shows how to make something. Some engineers show how to make a train. A plan can show how to make a ship, too.

Some engineers make computer programs.

What is the design process?

The design process is a set of steps. You follow them to solve a problem.

1. Find a Problem
2. Plan and Build
3. Test and Improve
4. Redesign
5. Communicate

One problem is that people walk in a garden. They step on flowers. What can you make to protect the flowers? How can you test what you make? How can you make it better?

This sign might help solve the problem.

You can keep a record of what you do. Write ideas in a notebook. Use a computer to make a plan. Use a tape recorder, too. Then you can listen to your work. A video camera can help, too. It takes moving pictures of your work.

Share what you make. Then you can write about it. You can help friends. Tell them about your plan.

A computer helps you to make and share a plan.

How can the design process help you solve a problem?

Follow these steps to solve a problem.

1. Find a Problem

   You and your classmates paint pictures. You put them on a shelf. They stick together.

2. Plan and Build

   You make a plan to hang them up. You build a clothesline.

3. Test and Improve

   Clip the pictures onto the clothesline. Paint drips to the floor. You need to improve your design so the paper lays flat.

Paintings take time to dry.

4. Redesign

   Try using two clotheslines. Clip each picture
   at the top and bottom. Make sure that the
   pictures face up. Now the paint does not drip!

5. Communicate

   Tell how you made it.

A clothesline helps solve
your problem. Two clotheslines
are even better.

Make a List

Work with a partner. Act out using something that is in your classroom. Have your partner guess its name. Take turns. Make a list. Next to each item, write how it solves a problem.

Research and Write

Work with a partner. Research jobs that engineers do. Use books or the Internet. Choose your favorite job. Make a poster. Draw a picture. Write about the job. Tell how an engineer solves one problem.